Mr. Greedy's Guide to FOOD

Written by Adam Hargreaves and Andrew Langley
Illustrated by Adam Hargreaves

Published in Great Britain by Egmont World Limited,
a division of Egmont Holding Limited,
Deanway Technology Centre, Wilmslow Road, Handforth,
Cheshire SK9 3FB, UK.

Printed in Italy

ISBN 0 7498 4890 1

Mr. Greedy's
pizza order.

The extra
anchovies
just tipped
the balance.

Mr. Busy

From an early age, Mr. Greedy had learned not to believe everything you read in the papers.

Mr. Greedy

Tossing pancakes was a skill that had always eluded Mr. Bump.

Mr. Bump

"What happened to
Mr. Greedy?"

"He's suffered
a snack attack!"

Mr. Greedy

"Waiter! There's a fly in my soup!"
Mr. Small

Mr. Jelly

Mr. Greedy

It's traditional for barbecues
to be accompanied by rain.

"YOU ARE WHAT YOU EAT."

It is generally thought to be impolite to speak with your mouth full.

Mr. Fussy

Mr. Chatterbox

As Mr. Clumsy left the restaurant he began to have doubts whether the cheese fondue had been such a wise choice.

"What a bouquet.
Peaches and cinnamon,
with a hint of lemon zest.
What can you smell,
Mr. Dizzy?"

"Grapes?"

Mr. Nosey

Mr. Dizzy

FOOD FOR THOUGHT

JUNK FOOD

Mr. Messy

It is important to remember to chew your food properly.

Mr. Skinny

Mr. Nosey

Mr. Small would become noticeably nervous whenever Mr. Greedy started talking about cherry tomatoes.

Mr. Small

The thought of meeting the presenter of her new cookery show kept Little Miss Shy awake at nights.

Little Miss Scatterbrain
asked permission
to get down from
the table.

Little Miss Scatterbrain

ALL YOU CAN EAT!
ALL WELCOME!
except for large pink men
Mr. Greedy

On a recent visit to London, Mr. Greedy discovered that there was a god after all.
HARRODS
FOOD
HALL
Mr. Greedy

A FRIDGE TOO FAR
Mr. Greedy

Keeping his elbows off the table was a dilemma that had plagued Mr. Tickle since childhood.

Mr. Tickle

The miscalculation that ruined Mr. Greedy's Christmas.

Mr. Greedy

THE 3 STAGES OF DIETING

"I've told you before, not to eat suites between meals."

"We have skimmed latte, mocha latte, ristretto, expresso, grande expresso, cappuccino, mocha frappé, iced latte ..."

"One extra-frothy cappuccino coming up."
Mr. Silly

“Oh look - Mr. Wrong’s new restaurant.”

Mr. Wrong

Mr. Greedy

"They say that inside every fat person, there is a thin person trying to get out."

"Well, unless his name is Houdini I don't think we'll be seeing him."

"Looks like the mice are on a diet again."
Mr. Small
Mr. Happy

A BALANCED DIET
Mr. Greedy

"I'm not sure Mr. Muddle's
Beef Wellington works very well ..."

Mr. Happy

Little Miss Sunshine

FAST FOOD
Mr. Rush
"Served in a
stale pun!"

"What is it?"
"Arabic Alphabet Soup!"
Mr. Silly

“Hmmm, it tastes just like my mother used to open.”

"It's a new concept. The fish choose the customers."
Mr. Silly
Little Miss Tiny

"Typical men. They're like bees round a honey pot!"

RECIPES
FOR
DISASTER
Mr. Muddle

Mr. Dizzy

Leftovers are an unknown phenomenon in Mr. Greedy's house.

"WHO ATE ALL THE PIES?"

Mr. Greedy

"I believe he has a nose for a good wine!"
Mr. Happy
Mr. Nosey

You can't make an omelette without breaking a few eggs.

Mr. Clumsy

LEAN CUISINE

Mr. Lazy

To avoid embarrassment, always check with the restaurant.

Some have a strict dress code.

TOO MANY COOKS SPOIL THE BROTH
Mr. Worry began to regret inviting
Miss Stubborn, Mr. Fussy and Miss Bossy.

Read through the recipe carefully before you begin cooking.
Mr. Wrong

Never be afraid to complain if you are dissatisfied with the service or food.

Mr. Grumpy

LOW
FAT
DIET
Mr. Greedy

CHOUX PASTRY

Mr. Nonsense

WEIGHT WATCHING

Mr. Nosey

"Soup ... no no, prawn cocktail ... no no, avocado ... no, pâté ... oh no, umm ... melon and parma ham ... no no, ummm, soup ... no, prawn cocktail ..."

Little Miss Fickle

"Bah, humbug!"
Mr. Grumpy

IF YOU CAN'T STAND THE HEAT,
GET OUT OF THE KITCHEN!

Mr. Snow

Steak sometimes requires gentle pounding to make it tender.

Mr. Strong

"WAITER.
Another banana please.
This one is bent."
Mr. Fussy

There was something not quite right about Mr. Topsy-Turvy's midnight feast.

"No, no, Mr. Muddle! I told you to fry it in your WOK!"